Wild Party

WILDE FAMILY

Read more about the Wilde Family in ...

Wilde Day Out
Wilde Style
Running Wilde
Wilde Child
Wilde Ride

Other series by Jenny Oldfield:

Definitely Daisy
Totally Tom
Horses of Half-Moon Ranch
My Little Life
Home Farm Twins
The Dreamseeker Trilogy

The WILDE FAMILY

Wilde Party

by Jenny Oldfield

illustrated by Sarah Nayler

Hodder
Children's
Books

a division of Hodder Headline Limited

Thanks to all the *wild* kids who have told me
jokes and funny stories during my visits
to schools and libraries

Text copyright © Jenny Oldfield 2004
Illustrations copyright © Sarah Nayler 2004

First published in Great Britain in 2004
by Hodder Children's Books

A Catalogue record for this book is available from
the British Library.

ISBN 0 340 87323 X

Printed and bound in Great Britain by Bookmarque Ltd, Croydon

The paper and board used in this paperback by Hodder Children's
Books are natural recyclable products made from wood grown in
sustainable forests. The manufacturing processes conform to the
environmental regulations of the country of origin.

Hodder Children's Books
a division of Hodder Headline Ltd
338 Euston Road
London NW1 3BH

One

The Cake! *The Cake!!*

It sat on the Wilde family's kitchen table, a shimmering chocolate treat for the twins' eleventh birthday. Two layers of sponge cemented together with butter icing, topped with chocolate.

'It couldn't be more chocolatey if we'd tried!' Jade sighed.

'Stand back!' Kayleigh warned. 'Jade, don't lean – on – the – table!'

The table tipped under Jade's weight and the cake slid towards the edge. Quick as a flash, Deanne nipped in and caught it before it fell. A splodge of soft icing landed on the floor.

'Whoops!' Jade giggled.

'How old are you?' Kayleigh snorted. 'Aren't you supposed to be nine years old, not nine months?'

Bop-bop-whop! Baby Kyle banged his plastic spoon on his tray.

Fussily Kayleigh set about smoothing the rippled icing with a warm, wet knife. 'It's taken me all morning to make this cake,' she reminded Jade.

'For *us* to make it!' Jade protested. 'Deanne and me helped, remember!'

Kayleigh smoothed and sniffed. 'Yeah, you went to the shop for the chocolate. But who was it who mixed the flour into the butter, sugar and egg mix? Who put it into the oven and timed it? Who made the butter icing ... ?'

'Yeah, yeah, yeah!' Jade yawned. She took the mixing bowl from the draining board and dredged out the very last remnants of raw cake mix with her finger. Meanwhile, little sis Deanne scooped out the remains of the icing bowl.

Bop-bop-wham! Kyle demanded his share of the leftovers. He opened his mouth wide and let out a hungry shriek.

'Good job Krystal and Carmel went birthday shopping with Mum,' Kayleigh pointed out. The cake was meant to be a secret, along with the party. If the twins had been around, it would have been hard to keep them out of the kitchen all morning. 'D'you think we should put Happy Birthday on the top?' she asked.

Jade and Deanne stood back to study the cake. It was good and deep, with masses of icing. True, it wasn't very even – up at one side and down at the other – and somehow crumbs had got mixed up with the smooth chocolate coating, but still it looked scrummy.

'Yes,' Deanne decided. 'Let's do Happy Birthday!'

Jade shook her head doubtfully.

'Waaagh!' Kyle cried from his high chair.

'H-a-p-y B-i-r-t-h-d-a-y!' Nervously Kayleigh squeezed the words through the icing tube on to the cake. Then she breathed a sigh of relief and put down her tools.

'Cool!' Jade nodded. Kayleigh had done better than she'd expected – the letters sloped, but only a bit, and the 'd-a-y' in 'Birthday' was squished together. But so what?

Deanne frowned. 'Doesn't "Happy" have two "p"s?'

'Oh, no!' Kayleigh shrieked and wailed
when she realized what she'd done. 'I'm
so thick! Why didn't you stop me? God,
they're gonna think I'm an idiot. We'll
have to scrap the whole thing!'

'No we won't,' Jade argued. 'Don't
worry, Krystal and Carmel won't notice.'

'But *I* will!' Kayleigh cried.

'Sorry.' Deanne felt it was her fault
for spotting the mistake.

'OK then, squeeze an extra "p" in,'
Jade suggested wearily. She could see
that Kayleigh was going off on one of
her strops.

'Don't be stupid!'

'Or put a candle plonk on top of the
mistake, so no one sees it.'

'Dummy!' Kayleigh seethed. 'No,
we'll have to start over.'

She was about to sweep the poor
cake off the table into the bin when
Jade stepped forward. 'No time. Take a
look at your watch. Carmel and Krystal
are due back in half an hour.'

Kayleigh groaned and checked the time. 'It's not fair – why does everything have to go wrong?'

'It's only one tiny little "p"!' Jade pointed out, trying not to smile.

Kayleigh disagreed. She frowned at the slanting, crumby, mis-spelt cake. 'It's a disaster. Look at it – it's awful!'

'It's yummy!' Deanne soothed.

'And here come the twins now!' Jade cried, spying them through the window and leaping across the kitchen towards the door. 'Quick, put the cake away before they get here!'

'Oh, no!' Kayleigh panicked. 'They're early. Get out there, Jade, and stop them coming in.'

'How?'

'I dunno. Just go!' Kayleigh shrieked.

Jade shot outside. 'Keep your hair on,' she muttered. Honestly, Kayleigh was such a drama queen these days. And Jade could swear it was worse since she'd started going out with Justin.

'OK, Deanne, stop Kyle from screaming the house down!' Kayleigh got a grip and began slinging things into the dishwasher. 'I'll hide the evidence.'

'Here, Kyley-wyley!' Deanne offered the baby the scrapings of the icing bowl.

'Waaagh-yummm!' He smacked his lips and demanded more.

Kayleigh wiped the surfaces and opened the window to let out cake smells. 'This has got to be one big surprise!' she muttered. 'Krystal and Carmel mustn't know a thing about it.'

'Here Kyley, try this.' Deanne offered the squawking baby a dollop of butter icing.

'Waagh-yummmm!'

'It's just my luck that they came back early,' Kayleigh moaned. She took the cake from the table and looked round for a good place to hide it. Somewhere that wasn't obvious - not the cupboard with the biscuit tin; that would be the first place the twins would head for when they got in ...

'Waaagh!' Kyle yelled as the taste of chocolate wore off.

Deanne lifted him out of his chair and plonked him on the floor.

Freedom! The baby tucked one fat leg under his bum and shuffled sideways like a crab. Then he tilted on to all fours and crawled pell-mell for the hallway.

'Stop him!' Kayleigh bawled. 'Wipe the chocolate off his face. Change his T-shirt. Watch it, or he'll ruin everything!'

'Hiya!' Jade appeared on the front lawn wearing a broad, blank grin.

'What's up with you?' Krystal asked.

She and Carmel were loaded with carrier bags and followed by an exhausted Mum. 'Put the kettle on, someone!' Mum sighed.

Obligingly Carmel swerved towards the side of the house and the kitchen door.

'No-o-oh!' Jade gasped, quickly cutting her off. 'Come upstairs and show me your stuff. You too, Krystal. I want to see what you bought!'

Easily waylaid, Carmel and Krystal followed Jade in through the front door.

'Thanks for that, Jade,' Mum sighed.

'I got a mega top,' Krystal told Jade, leaping upstairs and bursting into her bedroom. She flung her bags on to the bed. 'It's like the one Mia wears in the latest Dance Klub video. Du-dah!'

'Cool!' Jade nodded and whistled as Krystal pulled out a bright pink top with one tied shoulder strap. She could picture Krystal doing karaoke to her favourite Dance Klub hit single in that top. 'What did you get, Carmel?'

'Du-dah!' Carmel produced a teeny-weeny denim skirt.

'Give us a twirl,' Jade said. If they started trying things on, it should give Kayleigh tons of time to clear the kitchen.

Carmel eyed her suspiciously. 'How come you're so interested?' she demanded. 'You're the one who hates clothes, remember!'

Jade shrugged, then practised a handstand against the closed door. 'Please yourself.'

'I got these trousers to go with the top,' Krystal gushed. 'And new trainers. They were a present from the money Gran gave me.'

'I got a white shirt that ties at the waist and new flowery flip-flops,' Carmel joined in.

'Try 'em on,' Jade said again.

And this time they did.

'Gran, can you come
early this afternoon?'
Kayleigh had hidden
The Cake in the
bottom cupboard of
the bookcase in the

telly room. The dishwasher was swishing
away. The kitchen was tidy and Deanne
was making Mum a cuppa.

'Speak up, chickadee,' Gran
chirruped down the phone.

'I said, can you come early?' Kayleigh
hissed. 'We said four, but Krystal and
Carmel are back sooner than we thought.
Can you make it three o'clock instead?'

'Why are you whispering? Did you say
three? Let me see, I was meant to be
meeting Gordon and Alan for a game of
tennis, but I expect I can put that off.
Yes, chick – make that three!'

Click. The phone went dead.

Kayleigh sighed. Their gran had a

better social life than she did.

'Justin, I know you're working this morning, but will you be free for three o'clock?' Kayleigh's next call was to her boyfriend.

Then to Krystal's friends, Amanda and Jo-jo, and then Carmel's partners in crime, Holly and Rosanna. They all agreed to come to the party early.

'That's good. I don't think we could possibly keep the secret much later than that,' Mum said when Kayleigh explained the change of plan. 'Honestly, you should have heard them this morning, drifting into every shop in town, going on about not having a party this year. It was heart-rending, believe me!'

Kayleigh tutted and nodded. 'Don't tell me! Anyway, never mind – the cake's done!' she announced. Safe and sound in the telly room, out of harm's way.

'No party!' Krystal said in disgust for the twentieth time that day. She stood in

front of her bedroom mirror judging the
effect of the pink top and white trousers
and trainers. 'Does this look better with
my hair up or down?'

'Up,' Carmel said.

'Down,' Jade disagreed.

'It doesn't matter, since there's no
party to wear them to,' Carmel grumbled.

Krystal picked up her hairbrush, held
it to her mouth like a microphone and
rehearsed her karaoke.

'Dance, dance the night away, It's
with you I'm gonna stay – Babe!'

Two steps to the left, one forward,
slip your left foot behind your right and
step diagonally – yeah!

'You've gotta wiggle your shoulders
and point at the camera as well,' Carmel
advised.

Krystal threw her a dirty look. 'What
are you, my corry – coro – chory-thingy!'

'Yeah, your dance director!' Carmel
giggled.

'Choreographer,' Deanne added,

putting her head around the door. 'Cool clothes!' she grinned.

'Scoot and look after Kyle!' they told her with one voice.

Deanne scampered back downstairs.

'Brainbox!' Carmel grumbled. At seven, Deanne was already far more clever than any normal kid should be.

'Dance, dance to the beat, Feel the burn, feel the heat – Babe!'

Krystal sang, pointed and twirled – *bee-bop, boo-bop-a-loo!*

'How come we're not getting a party this year?' Carmel sighed. She twitched at her hair in the mirror, pushing it behind her ears, then pulling it in front again.

'Yeah, how come?' Krystal echoed, in between verses.

''Cos you're too old,' Jade fibbed. She looked them straight in the eyes and lied. Boy, was she good at this! 'You're not little kids any more.'

'That's not fair. Kayleigh had a party when she was eleven,' Krystal pointed out.

'That was different,' Jade shrugged.

'No, it's the same,' Carmel insisted. 'But we asked and they said no way. All we could have was birthday shopping with Mum.'

'Yeah, "I was eleven and all I got was this lousy T-shirt!"' Krystal quipped, pretending to scrawl the long logo across her chest.

Sitting cross-legged on the bed, Jade let the twins moan on. Little did they know, but there was a stack of blown-up, pink and white 'Happy Birthday' balloons tucked away in Kayleigh's room, and a compilation of birthday music on the CD player. Not to mention the gleaming, yummy-scrummy birthday cake that Kayleigh had made.

'Kyley!' Deanne sang out from the bottom of the stairs. She ran and peeped into the kitchen to see Mum sipping her tea, her feet up on a stool.

'Try the telly room,' Mum yawned.

Deanne scooted next door. 'Kyley-wyle!'
No reply.

Super-shuffler stopped dead behind the sofa and waited until Deanne disappeared. He listened carefully, then he launched himself at a rapid crawl round the side, past the TV, across the rug towards the bookcase.

Sniff-sniff!

Kyle's mouth watered, his blue eyes were round as saucers.

Sniff-sniff. The yummy choccy smell was coming from the cupboard. *Sniff!*

'Kyley!' Deanne trilled, skipping across the hall and peering into the cupboard under the stairs.

The baby drooled. His chubby fingers took hold of the cupboard handle and he pulled. The door opened and sent him sprawling backwards. But he wriggled and turned on to his tummy, making a second attack on the cupboard.

'Where are you, Kyle?' Deanne called.

Kyle stared at a chocolate dream

come true. He was inches away from
a whole, untouched, mouth-watering,
lip-smacking cake. All to himself, with
nobody looking. *Yummm!*

Deanne doubled back towards the telly
room to take another look.

Kyle reached forward with a trembling
hand. He splodged his palm down on
'Hapy', curled his fingers and grabbed a
handful of icing. Then another and
another. He didn't care if his hand missed
his mouth, or if the icing was smeared
over his face, in his hair, down his chest.
Lick, slurp, grab, guzzle.

Deanne appeared at the door. Her
mouth dropped open when she
saw the smashed, crumpled
cake and the baby oozing
chocolate.

'Oh, Kyle!' she wailed.
He looked round with
a burp and a smile.
Gulp, yummmm!

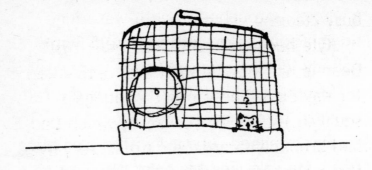

Two

'You'd think there'd been an earth-quake!' Jade told Perry Wade next door. She'd beaten a hasty retreat into the back garden to escape the fallout.

'I thought I heard screams,' Perry admitted. 'So did Hamlet. He hid under the bucket.'

'Who's Hamlet?'

'My new hamster. D'you wanna see him?'

Jade snuck a look over her shoulder to see if anyone was watching from the house. Being seen going off with geeky Perry wouldn't be good for her street

cred. But it was OK – they were still
busy clearing up the cake.

Kyle had splatted it flat, *gobble-gulp*,
Deanne had walked in on him and yelled
for Kayleigh. There'd been a mega
squawk, then a long screech, which Dad
had probably heard from his surgery over
the other side of town. It had brought
Krystal and Carmel thundering downstairs, but Jade had been super-quick
and cut them off before they'd reached
the telly room.

'Is Kayleigh dying?' Krystal had
quizzed. 'Did Justin dump her, or what?'

'Kyle just shredded her latest copy of
Teen Dream,' Jade had fibbed. Inspiration
had struck; she was getting better by the
minute. She'd even dug into her shorts
pocket and dragged out a pound. 'Better
go and buy her another,' she'd suggested.

Carmel had taken the money and
picked off the fluff. 'Why is it sticky?'
she'd asked, pulling a fussy face.

The shrieks had continued.

'Waaagh!' Kyle had wailed.

'Never mind, just go!' Jade had herded Carmel and Krystal out of the house. 'No need to rush,' she'd added.

The birthday girls had taken her advice and scarpered to the shop.

Now Jade was devising her own escape route.

Kayleigh had cried and snivelled, scooped up the wrecked cake and flung it in the bin. She'd blubbed some more. 'That's the last time I do anything for anyone!' she'd declared, then retired to her room in more floods of tears.

It was time to leave Mum and Deanne to jetwash Kyle and excavate chocolate icing out of the beige carpet, Jade had thought. Even talking to Perry was better than sticking around to help with that. 'What colour is Hamlet?' she asked him as they squeezed through the gap in the hedge into his garden.

'Chocolatey brown,' he answered.

*

'Go up and tell Kayleigh it's not the end of the world,' Mum told Deanne.

Deanne went upstairs with a trembling lip. 'It's not the end of the world,' she repeated, her eyes watering, her untidy fair hair sticking out at odd angles.

Kayleigh sat staring into her dressing-table mirror at her red-rimmed eyes and puffy face. 'I'm so ugly!' she moaned.

Deanne sat on the bed. 'No you're not.'

'I am. Look at my piggy eyes. And I hate my hair.'

'It's cool,' Deanne argued. 'You're really pretty.'

'I'm not. I'm horrible.' Piggy eyes and a too-big nose, like Dad's. And her hair was a naff, boring light brown and they wouldn't let her dye it proper blonde.

Deanne sighed and got up again. 'Justin doesn't think so.'

Kayleigh screwed up her face. 'He would if he saw me like this.'

There was a heavy silence as Deanne wandered away.

Justin? Suddenly Kayleigh broke out of her sulk. *Justin – Justin worked at Tesco's – Tesco's sold cakes. Birthday cakes. Yeah!*

'What else does he do?' Jade asked Perry.

They were in his garden shed, watching Hamlet trundle around inside his exercise wheel.

'He eats,' Perry told her.

'Big deal.'

'He stuffs food into his cheeks. They have big pouch things to store it in.'

'Sounds a bit like Kyle.' Jade stared at the little brown creature's fat face. Hamlet had beady black eyes and cute round ears. 'Not very exciting, is he?' she

commented. If she had a pet, it would
be a dog that could run really fast, or a
cat that could pounce and climb trees.

'D'you wanna hold him?' Perry offered.

'OK, then.'

So Perry opened the cage, picked the
hamster up and gave him to Jade.

She cupped him between her hands.
His fur was soft, his little feet were
hard, with sharp claws. 'Aaaah!' she
murmured.

Hamlet twitched his cute nose then
made a sudden leap for freedom. From
being a squishy, beanie-baby type, he
grew sleek and muscly, jumping clear of
Jade's hands on to a nearby shelf. Then
he scuttled behind a stack of plant pots
and came out beside an open bag of bird
feed. *Chomp-chomp* – he was one happy
hamster!

'Wow!' Jade was impressed. Maybe
there was more to him than met the
eye. 'That was fast!'

Perry slammed the shed door shut and

told her that hamsters had a reputation for running away. 'They're always breaking out of their cages and going on the rampage. Bo and Jez had one that ate the insides of their tumble-drier. They had to call the engineer to take the whole thing apart before they could get him free.'

'Wow!' Jade said again.

'You get long-haired ones and short-haired ones, golden ones and albinos with pink eyes ...' know-all Perry lectured.

'Yeah, yeah.' Gingerly Jade crept near and scooped Hamlet out of the bag of bird seed. 'Can I borrow him?' she asked.

'Dream on!'

'Go on!'

'No way!' End of discussion.

'You can come to our party this afternoon if you let me borrow Hamlet for one night!' she said after a long silence.

Perry narrowed his eyes and insisted on snatching the hamster and putting him into his wooden cage. 'Whose party?'

'Krystal and Carmel's.'

Scrabble-scrabble –
Hamlet wasn't happy.

'Thought they
weren't having a
party,' Perry muttered. 'I heard them
moaning about it on the way home from
school yesterday.'

Jade crouched down close to the
front of the cage. 'Well, they are, but
it's a secret,' she confided. 'Go on, Pez
– can I borrow him?'

Perry sniffed thoughtfully. 'Nope,' he
said.

Ding-dong!

The doorbell rang and Kayleigh nearly
jumped out of her skin.

Had the concealer she'd slapped on
under her eyes worked? Was her nose
still red? Too bad! She shot downstairs to
answer the door.

'Hiya,' Justin said, handing her a big
cardboard box.

'You saved my life!' she gushed. No more sulks, no more strops. 'Quick, come in before Krystal and Carmel get back!'

Grinning sheepishly, Justin followed her upstairs. 'I had to get this cake,' he told her, showing her a concoction in pink, red and orange – not a speck of chocolate in sight. 'I know it looks naff, but it was that or a Teletubby. It was all we had left.'

'Must be a big rush on birthday cakes,' Kayleigh simpered, taking the box and peeking inside. 'Oh, it's cool!'

'I brought candles as well.' Justin's trendy blond streaks glistened in the strong sunlight pouring through Kayleigh's window. A slight blush brought a glow to his tanned skin.

'You really did save my

life!' *Moron!* Kayleigh kicked herself for
repeating what she'd already said.

'I felt like a smuggler getting through customs,' Justin quipped. '"Tesco Employee Caught Cake-Running! A police spokesperson said it was the first case of its kind!"'

Kayleigh giggled and couldn't stop! *Idiot! It's not that funny.*

'Suppose I'd better be off then.' Justin shuffled towards the door while Kayleigh hid the cake in her wardrobe, which she locked in case Kyle came on the rampage again.

'You could stay,' she suggested. *He's gonna say no!* The second she said it, she wished she hadn't.

'No. Thanks. I've got to get back to work. I'm on my lunch break.'

'Oh yeah, right.' With a crestfallen look, she followed him downstairs.

'But I could come back later,' Justin blurted out. *She's gonna say no!* he thought.

'Cool!' Kayleigh said.

They hovered on the front doorstep. 'Come for the p-a-r-t-y,' she suggested after Justin had made a lunge for her hand. 'It starts at three, but you don't have to be here for the beginning.'

'I can make it by four,' he mumbled, moving in.

Kayleigh tilted her face up. He was so close his eyes were blurry, and then he was kissing her and she was floating on air.

'Corrrr!' Krystal yelled as she and Carmel barged in with a copy of *Teen Dream*.

'Snog-alert!' Carmel shrieked.

Exit Justin with a bright red face. In a flash, before Kayleigh could blow up, Jade whooshed the twins upstairs to their room. There was two hours to go before people started arriving for the party, and she, Jade, planned to keep them penned in while Mum, Deanne and Kayleigh got ready downstairs.

'Perry's got a hamster,' she told them.

'Wow!' Krystal said flatly, then yawned. As far as she was concerned, Perry Wade was a nerdy, geeky, weedy nobody.

Carmel asked her how she knew. 'You haven't been talking to the enemy, have you?'

'No. I heard his mum telling him to buy a bag of shavings for its cage,' Jade came back instantaneously. *Wowee-zowee, what a liar!* 'Bo and Jez lost their hamster inside their tumble dryer,' she informed them.

Carmel and Krystal eyed her suspiciously. 'Who told you?' Carmel asked.

Whoops! 'They did. Who wants to do my hair?' she asked, quickly sliding on to a different subject and sitting down on Carmel's bed. That should keep them happy for at least an hour.

'Me!' they both said, taking one side of Jade's head each.

'I'm doing teensy weeny plaits and making corn rows,' Krystal informed her.

'I'm gonna hotbrush and style it,' Carmel said. 'Let's make sure there's a proper parting down the middle.'

Ding-dong!

It was two o'clock, and Gran bounced in on Deanne, Mum and Kayleigh. Kyle sat in his high-chair eating strawberry jelly.

'Whoo-hooh!' Gran cried, dumping a basket full of sausage-rolls, cheese straws and three party packs of crisps on the kitchen table. 'Yes, I'm early, and yes, I knew you'd be in a last-minute panic. Where are the birthday girls?'

'Ssshh!' Kayleigh hissed. 'This is meant to be a surprise!'

Suck-slurp! Kyle sieved mashed-up jelly between his gums.

Mwah! Gran pounced and gave him a great big kiss.

Already laid out was a feast of sandwiches, chocolate fingers, savoury

snacks and of course, the cake. The
table groaned under the weight.

Gran was dressed for the occasion in a short, white top with tinselly strands knitted in, plus white cut-offs and silver flip-flops. She wore giant daisy earrings and a bright red bandanna in her short blonde hair.

'You look lovely, Gran,' Deanne told her.

Mwah! Gran pounced again. 'Come upstairs and I'll help you get dressed,' she suggested.

Trotting along after her, Deanne was telling Gran that her invisible friend, Buggle-mug, had been called to his home planet to celebrate his own birthday. 'Like ET,' she explained.

'Ah yes, Buggle-mug,' Gran said with a twinkle in her eye. 'How old is he?'

'Three hundred,' Deanne said gravely. 'That equals ten in human years. They have thirty birthdays for every one we have. Thirty lots of cards and presents.'

'Lovely, dear, Gran murmured, doing her best to tiptoe quietly along the first-floor landing so as not to disturb the twins on the floor above. The boards creaked as she went.

'Hi, Gran!' Carmel and Krystal's door flew open and they burst out. Jade followed with half a head plaited, the other half hotbrushed, styled and sprayed.

'Thirty parties and thirty birthday cakes,' Deanne went on dreamily.

'What party?' Krystal demanded.

'What birthday cake?' Carmel quizzed.

They had razor-sharp hearing and in-built radar for working out secrets. Poised on the top landing in their birthday clothes, they fizzed with suspicious excitement.

'Nothing!' Gran trilled. 'Ignore us. We're just chatting.'

'What are you doing with Deanne?' Carmel persisted.

'Yeah, Gran, and why are you here, all dressed up like that?' Krystal asked.

Gran beamed up at them, then advanced upstairs, arms spread wide. 'To wish you a happy birthday and to give you a big hug and a kiss!'

Yuck! Anything but that! Quicker than Concorde, Krystal and Carmel zoomed back into their rooms.

Three

'Golly-gosh, whose birthday is it?' Dad joked when he came home from work.

Pink and white balloons filled the kitchen and telly room. Big banners were pinned on to the walls.

Deanne grinned. 'Carmel and Krystal still don't know about the p-a-r-t-y!' she whispered. 'They're upstairs with Jade, playing Dance Klub's latest CD.'

'Dad, go and get changed,' Kayleigh ordered. 'We're nearly ready to start.'

While the twins had been holed up in their room, the party planners had been hard at work. Gran had helped Kayleigh

set up a disco in the telly room, Deanne
had put out party poppers and Mum had
dressed Kyle in cute denims.

'Why do I have to get changed?' Dad
protested as Kayleigh propelled him
upstairs.

''Cos you do!' It was time for Kayleigh
herself to get glammed up. She shot up
to her room, threw open the door of her
wardrobe and began to pick her outfit.

Stone-washed denims, white top and
moccasins? Black combats with orange
T-shirt and silver-grey trainers? She tried
on one after the other, chucking stuff on
the floor. 'Yuck! ... Ergh! ... No way!'

OK, this is serious! Surrounded by
cast-offs, hot and sticky, Kayleigh was
getting desperate. *Justin's gonna be here
later!* she reminded herself. *I've gotta
look good!*

She grabbed another pair of trousers
and wriggled into them. 'Do these make
my legs look stumpy?' she asked, dashing
into the twins' room.

'Yep,' Krystal said, without looking round. She, Carmel and Jade were rehearsing more dance moves.

'Oh no, I've got mega-short legs!' Kayleigh wailed as she caught sight of herself in the mirror.

'Look at it this way, Don't care what you say, I'm gonna dance the night awa-ay!' Carmel mimed to a Dance Klub track while Kayleigh ran away in despair.

'Why's she spending so much time on what she wears?' Krystal wondered. 'Is she going out?'

Jade nodded. 'She's arranged to meet Justin outside Tesco's when he finishes work.' *Whuh!* Another fib made its entrance, smooth as anything. At this rate, she'd get into the Guinness Book of Records for Most Lies by a Nine Year Old Without Being Found Out.

The track finished and Carmel flopped down on the bed. 'I'm bored!' she groaned.

'Let's go out,' Krystal suggested.

'Nothing's happening here – no *party*, or anything!' She went out on to the landing and shouted this loud enough for everyone to hear.

Her remark was met by a resounding silence.

'Yeah, let's go,' Carmel agreed.

Jade vaulted the banister and landed on the stairs. 'No! You can't go!' she yelled, blocking their way.

Carmel and Krystal frowned down at her. 'Why not?'

''Cos – 'cos I want to show you how long I can stand on my head for!' Jade bundled them back into their room and slammed the door.

Carmel curled her lip. 'That's about as exciting as watching paint dry.'

Krystal yawned and fiddled with her hair in the mirror. 'C'mon, let's go,' she said again.

'Where to? You can't!' Jade cried, standing on her head in front of the door. 'One-and-two-and-three-and ...'

'Big deal!' Carmel glanced out of the window and thought she saw Holly and Rosanna walking up the street. She banged hard and waved to attract their attention, but her two friends ducked down behind a hedge. 'Weird!' she muttered, with a shake of her head.

'Ten-eleven-twelve ...' Jade counted, feeling the blood rush to her head.

'Come in, quick!' Deanne hissed at Holly and Rosanna, who had waited behind the hedge until the coast was clear.

'I think Carmel saw us!' Holly whispered, sneaking in the back door. She and Rosanna had gone along with this plan to keep the party secret by acting dead casual as they'd given the twins their cards and pressies the day before.

'Doing anything spesh for your birthdays?' Rosanna had asked Carmel.

'Going shopping,' Carmel had replied with a laid-back shrug.

'What, no party?' Holly had said, rolling her eyes and tutting.

Rosanna had almost giggled and given it away.

Now they crept into the house, spray-gelled and accessorized with silvery scrunchies, bangles and bright pink nail polish.

'Wow!' they said when they went in the kitchen and saw the sarnies, crisps, sausages ... and the pink, orange and red cake.

'Kayleigh made a chocolate one, but Kyle ate it,' Deanne explained sadly.

'Waaagh!' Kyle cried from his high chair.

'Aah, sweet!' Rosanna cried, rushing to coo over the trendy denim baby with the blond, fluffy hair.

Then Amanda and Jo-jo arrived and compared outfits with Rosanna and Holly. How much did that cost? Where did you get it? I bought one like that from Top Shop.

'Waaaaagh!' Kyle protested.

'Aah, look!' Jo-jo chucked him under his fat chin. 'He's got four teeth!' She picked him up and staggered under his weight.

Mum came downstairs in her new fawn suede shirt and cream trousers. 'Are we all here?' she asked nervously.

'Except Dad and Kayleigh,' Deanne told her. 'And Jade. She's standing on her head so the twins can't get out of their room.'

'She's doing a great job,' Mum said, anxiously looking at her watch.

'Eighty-three – eighty-four – eighty-five ...' Jade gasped. By now she was the colour of a beetroot.

'Dad, let us out!' Carmel cried when

she heard heavy footsteps on the landing. 'Jade's blocking our door!'

'Candle in the wind,' Dad hummed loudly. 'Never knowin' who to turn to when the rain came in ... I would've liked to know you ...'

'Rats!' Krystal frowned. 'Jade, we want to go out!' she bellowed, bending down and getting close as she could to Jade's right eardrum.

'Are we ready?' Gran asked as Dad joined the group in the kitchen. Balloons bobbed around her head. One burst on the spiky petal of her earring. Gran jumped and shrieked.

'Sssshhhh!' everyone warned, hands to their lips.

At that point, Jo-jo gave in and put squirming Kyle down on the floor. He set off at the speed of light towards the food.

'Kayleigh's still not here!' Deanne insisted. 'I'll go and fetch her.'

She found her oldest sister sitting
sniffing on her bed.

'What am I gonna wear?' Kayleigh
wailed, surrounded by a mountain of
cast-off clothes.

'You look great in what you've got
on,' Deanne assured her. Lime-green
crop-top, navy blue combats and white
trainers. 'Everyone's waiting for you.'

Kayleigh stood up and turned sideways
to stare at herself in the mirror. 'I can't
go down looking like this!'

Deanne sighed. 'Shall I tell them
you're not coming to the p-a-r-t-y?'

'Ssssh! Yes. No. I'm on my way!'
Quickly Kayleigh zapped her hair up into
a high ponytail, tugged at her crop-top
and shot out of the door.

'Kayleigh, let us out!' Krystal cried
from inside the twins' room.

'A hundred and one, a hundred and
two, a hundred and three ...' Jade droned.

Downstairs, Dad rugby-tackled Kyle
just before he reached the sausages

on a low table by the window.

'Close!' Mum gasped.

'Ready?' Gran asked, her hand poised over the CD player.

Mum, Dad, Kayleigh, Deanne, Kyle, Amanda, Jo-jo, Holly and Rosanna were crammed into the telly room.

'Ready!' Kayleigh agreed. She held open the door so that sound would carry up the stairs.

Gran pressed a button.

'You're the best, you're the best, In the north, south, east and west, You're the very best!' Dance Klub belted out their all-time, mega number one hit.

'One hundred and fifty-nine, one hundred and sixty ...' Up in the twins' room, Jade heard the pre-arranged cue. She collapsed in a heap on the carpet. 'OK, you can go now,' she gasped at Carmel and Krystal.

Krystal elbowed Carmel to one side then stepped over Jade. 'What's going on?' she yelled from the landing.

'You're my girl, you're my girl, My diamond, my precious pearl, You're the very best!'

Krystal leaped over Jade's exhausted body. 'Let's go see!'

Almost falling over themselves, they scrambled downstairs.

At the thunder of footsteps, Gran took down the volume. 'One-two-three!' she cued.

A deep breath, then everyone started up. 'Happy Birthday to you!'

For a nano-second Krystal and Carmel paused to look at one another.

'Happy Birthday to you, Happy Birthday, de-ar ...'

The twins gasped and flew down the rest of the stairs. They burst through the hall then stopped dead at the telly room door. There was a cloud of pink and white balloons, a row of grinning faces – and Kyle screaming blue murder.

'... Car-mel and Krys-tal, Happy Birthday to you! *Waaaaa-aaaagh!*'

'Wow, cool!' Krystal beamed.

'Cool!' Carmel echoed.

'Surprise!' everyone yelled, dragging the twins in while Gran turned up the volume on 'You're The Best'.

The birthday girls whooped and danced to the beat. They grabbed balloons and whopped each other over the head. 'This is mega!' they cried.

Staggering down after her marathon headstand, Jade crowed over the part she'd played in keeping the secret. 'I never thought I was gonna make it past a hundred and ten,' she told Deanne and Kayleigh. 'My head went tingly. It felt like my brain was gonna burst!'

'Yuck!' Deanne grimaced.

Kayleigh curled her top lip. 'Gross!'

'But I did it. And Krystal and Carmel never suspected a thing!' The

effort had made Jade thirsty, so she led
the way into the kitchen for a drink.

'You're the very best!' Dance Klub
warbled while Carmel and Krystal jigged
and bopped under the cloud of balloons.

Bop-whop-bee-bop-a-lop! They twirled
and battered each other with their
balloons, then let their jaws drop open
when they spotted the food.

'Tuck in.' Mum gave the word, and
the locusts descended. The party guests
piled their plates high with sausage
rolls, cheese and onion crisps, chocolate
fingers and jellybeans.

'Aagh-waagh!' Kyle cried, until Jo-jo
stuck a chocolate finger in his fist. He
attacked it with his four teeth.

Then, all around, there was the sound
of frantic munching and crunching,
sucking, slurping and chewing. Music
played on in the background. Mum lit the
candles on the cake. The party girls were
happy.

Four

'Thank you, Mum! Thank you, Dad!'
Krystal and Carmel sang as they blew out
the candles then slurped 7-Up. 'This is the
coolest birthday we've ever had! You're
the best, you're the best, dah-dah!'

'How about thanking *us*?' Jade
demanded, her mouth full of icing.

'Yeah – er – thanks,' Krystal mumbled.
Thanking your own sisters didn't come
easily.

Meanwhile, Rosanna, Holly, Jo-jo and
Amanda stuffed themselves and Kyle with
cake.

'Hey, did I just see Perry Wade sneaking

into our garden?' Carmel mentioned above the noise of the party. She went to the kitchen window and looked out.
'Nope. Must've been seeing things.'

'Party-party!' Jo-jo cried, picking Kyle up and dancing with him.

'Don't make him puke!' Amanda warned.

'Let's play some games,' Krystal suggested, leading the way back into the telly room. 'How about musical cushions?'

'No. I want pass the parcel,' Carmel demanded. It had been her favourite game when she was a little kid – passing the bulky parcel and ripping off a layer of paper when the music stopped, the parcel getting smaller and smaller, hoping that you were going to be the last one to open it and win the Mars Bar inside.

'Musical cushions!' Krystal insisted, grabbing cushions from the sofa and spreading them across the floor.

'Count me out.' Kayleigh knew she would muss up her hair and crease her trousers if she joined in. 'I'll do the music.'

The rest waited for the CD to begin, then romped around the room, poised to drop on to the nearest cushion. Kayleigh would make as if to press the pause button, then lift her hand, fake it again, then grin as Holly or Amanda plonked on to a cushion. The girls got up with an embarrassed smile. Then at last, Kayleigh did pause the music for real. Elbows jostled, feet tripped, bodies lurched and bumped on to the floor.

'Krystal, you're out!' Carmel claimed as she fought her sister for the last spare cushion.

Krystal clawed it back. 'I'm so not!'

'You so are!'

'Not!' The tug of war went on.

'Call it a trial run,' Gran suggested. 'It's a tester. So this time no one's out.'

The girls all got back on their feet and twirled around the room again, letting the grown-ups and Kyle retreat to the kitchen for cups of tea.

Da-di-dah-di-dah! Silence. *Plonk!*

'Amanda, you're out!' Tricky-finger Kayleigh cried.

Da-da-dah-di-dah. Dum-de-dum, did-dle-dum! Silence. There was a squeal as Deanne dived for a cushion and missed.

'You're out,' Kayleigh told her, no messing.

Gradually the numbers were going down. Rosanna went next, then Jo-jo. Which left Krystal, Carmel, Jade and Holly cavorting around the room like bright, jerky cartoon figures. Kayleigh's finger hovered over the pause button.

'Perry!' The music played on, but Jade stopped mid-twirl. This time she'd definitely seen their neighbour's face at the window. He'd squished his nose up against the pane and was pulling a stupid face.

Holly, Krystal and Carmel continued to dance.

Soon more faces appeared. There were Bo and Jez, Mark, James and Danny, ganging up behind Perry and peering in. In fact, it was the whole five-a-side football team from the park, their hair sticking up in bad quiffs, their faces split by broad, jeering grins.

Da-da-dum-di-dah! Kayleigh forgot the button and stared at the huddle of boys.

'C'mon, Kayleigh, stop the music!' Carmel cried, her back to the window, poised to pounce on to a cushion.

But Kayleigh pointed at the party poopers. 'Boys!' she muttered. Slowly everyone in the room turned to see them.

'Let us in!' Perry whooped. 'We wanna come to the party!'

Carmel and Krystal approached the window, hands on hips. 'Get lost, Perry!'

'Whoo-oooh!' the soccer players scoffed. They were obviously enjoying crashing the twins' birthday bash. 'Perry said we were all invited!'

'No way!' Carmel stood her ground. She flung open the window and argued back. 'This is a private party. Anyway, it was a secret. How did you know about it?'

Uh-oh! Jade backed behind the sofa and tried to become invisible. She might have known it was a major mistake to give anything away to Perry Wade – even the time of day. But at that point she'd been too intent on borrowing his hamster to be on her guard.

Perry came straight out with it, like she knew he would. 'Jade told me,' he said.

Jade screwed up her eyes and mouth. Wait for it.

Carmel and Krystal turned on her like she was the worst traitor. 'You told Perry about our secret party!' they cried, as with one voice.

Jade squared her shoulders and tried

to tough it out. 'OK, yeah, I did. So?'

'Well now they're here and we can't get rid of them,' Krystal wailed.

'We'll climb in through the window if you don't open the door,' Danny laughed. 'We want to party, party, party!'

'See!' Carmel groaned.

'Party, party!' the gang at the window chorused. 'We shall not, we shall not be moved!'

It was Jo-jo who spoke up above the racket. 'Why not let them in?' she asked.

There was a loud gasp from Krystal and Carmel, as if Jo-jo had let out a bad swear word.

'That's 'cos she fancies Danny!' Holly snickered.

Jo-jo slapped her hand over Holly's mouth. 'You're dead!' she warned. 'Anyway, you fancy Perry!'

'Perry!' Amanda and Rosanna nearly died laughing.

'No way!' Krystal and Carmel refused to budge. This was their party. They were in charge.

'We shall not be moved!' The boys sang and clamoured at the window.

Then Gran opened the kitchen door and stepped out. 'Come in, boys!' she said cheerily. 'There's plenty of food left. I'm sure you can help us polish it off!'

'Don't even ask!' Jade had decided on a hasty retreat. She'd watched Perry and co. take fistfuls of peanuts and popcorn while Krystal and Carmel had sulked big time. The invasion of the soccer team plus geeky Perry was *so* not cool.

And who had got the blame? Jade!

So she'd sneaked off while the boys scoffed and the girls twittered in a corner. And now she was in Perry's garden shed talking to the hamster.

'You don't need to tell me – I know I

should be at the party, but what would you do if two of your sisters told you you were dead and they'd drop you in it with your mum and dad about the time last Tuesday when you didn't do your maths homework and you copied your best mate's and your teacher found out and you had to beg with him not to tell your parents?'

It was a long, complex question that didn't stop Hamlet from trundling away in the exercise wheel inside his cage. The wheel creaked and Hamlet puffed.

Jade filled in the answer herself. 'I'll tell you what you'd do. You'd scarper and wait for them to calm down. Which is what I'm doing in your shed. Waiting for Carmel and Krystal to forget it was me who told Perry about the party. It wasn't a smart move, I know that now. I mean, they hate Perry, and yeah, I know Perry's your owner and he feeds you and cleans you out, but he's never usually nice to us Wildes.'

Hamlet wheezed and ground to a halt. He crept out of his wheel and came to the edge of the cage to peer out at Jade. He fixed her with his beady black eyes.

'You know what I mean?' Jade asked.

Hamlet sat on his hind legs, squishy as a beanie baby, his front paws dangling. He twitched his nose and whiskers.

'D'you want a peanut?' Jade asked, fumbling in her pocket amongst her stash of jellybeans and Rolos. After all, there was no point in risking going hungry when she bailed out of the party.

Hamlet sniffed then scrabbled excitedly at the wire mesh. *Food. At long last!*

The boys ate and the girls sulked.

'They only came for the nosh,' Amanda grunted.

'Yeah, and to annoy us,' Rosanna added.

In the telly room the last track on the CD played and no one bothered to put on a new one. A few balloons drifted into the hall and bounced gently off Kyle's head.

'Come here, Kyle!' Kayleigh called – sensible big sis ignoring both Perry's raucous gang and Carmel and Krystal's drama queen sulks. She picked the baby up, careful not to get melted chocolate on her crop-top.

'What we need is more music!' Gran decided, seeing that the party had suddenly fallen flat. She skipped through the balloons and picked up a disc messily labelled 'Carmel and Krystal's Dance ~~compa~~ ~~compar~~ compilation'. 'This is the one!' she cried, sliding it into the player.

'And this is DJ Gran Wilde, coming to you from Radio Hartland, the voice of Hartsbridge, with all the latest dance tracks from your favourite rave bands!' she began.

Krystal and Carmel almost died of embarrassment.

A track by Boys R Us blared out as Gran turned up the volume. 'Groovy, baby!' she cried, doing a jiggling dance in time to the music.

Rosanna and Holly giggled, then decided to join in. At first they had the whole room to themselves, then Amanda made three. Soon a couple of the boys drifted in from the kitchen to watch.

'Tell me this isn't happening!' Krystal wailed.

Carmel spotted Jo-jo sidling up to Danny and dragging him on to the dance floor, the traitor!

Danny resisted, then shrugged, ran a hand through his quiff and started to dance.

'And that was Boys R Us with their last but one hit single, from their Christmas album "Dance Crazy"!' Gran announced as the track faded.

'How did she know that?' Amanda wondered.

'Hey, your gran's cool!' Holly added.

'Everybody dance!' Gran ordered, recognizing the lead-in to the next track. 'This is "While You Were

Sleeping" by Tanya!' she announced, her silvery accessories glistening in a low ray of sunlight that slanted across the room. 'It was a mega hit for her back in February this year!'

'Wanna dance?' Mark asked Kayleigh, who brushed him off with a superior look. 'OK, what about you?' he asked Holly.

Holly grinned and danced.

Then Rosanna and Amanda dragged Bo and Jez into a foursome.

That only left James and – ergh – Perry!

Carmel gulped and made a grab for James in the same split second as Krystal. They made a threesome and danced like crazy.

'I was awake while you were
sleeping, Too many lies and I was
weeping.'

The five-a-side boys swayed and
turned in their dirty, beat-up trainers
and muddy T-shirts. The party girls
glittered and shone.

'You wanna dance, Perry?' Deanne
asked quietly.

Perry looked down at his feet. 'I
don't know how,' he mumbled.

'Yes, you do!' Gran said, shooing him
from behind.

'Don't lie to me, baby, Don't you lie!'
Tanya warbled.

Everyone was dancing, Gran was
dee-jaying. In the kitchen, Kyle took a
nap on Dad's knee and Mum answered a
knock on the door.

'Kayleigh, Justin's here!' Mum called,
letting the visitor in.

The sound of his name sent a tingle
through Kayleigh and made a little knot
in her stomach. But she must be cool.

Taking a deep breath and trying not to rush, she made her way between the dancing couples.

Justin stood uncomfortably in the kitchen with the grown-ups. He watched Mrs Wilde clearing the party leftovers from the table, and little Kyle snoring on Mr Wilde's lap. Then Kayleigh made her entrance – a fresh vision of loveliness in lime-green and sparkling white, her hair in a high ponytail, looking dead casual.

Kayleigh's heartbeat quickened. Justin had changed out of his Tesco's uniform into a plain white T-shirt and jeans. His short blond hair had that trendy, messy look that she really liked. But, deep breaths – don't look too keen. 'Hiya,' she said shyly.

'Hiya,' he mumbled, flaming red to the roots of his hair. 'Is the party over?'

'No,' she said with a slow smile. *Now that you're here, it's only just begun!*

Five

'The Wilde household is really rocking!'
Gran's accent turned American as
she dee-jayed her way through the
afternoon. 'Let's get deep in the groove
now with Aaron Brown and "Throughout
The Night"!'

'The stars are out, the moon is
shining, Every cloud has a silver lining,
When you're with me, babe!'

Carmel jumped and jiggled, Krystal
made up a new routine, Deanne did her
own thing to the music. And by now the
boys had loosened up and were inventing
cool moves on the dance floor.

'Look at Jez – he thinks he's still playing footie!' Rosanna giggled.

Holly grinned. 'What about Bo? He looks like he should be on a skateboard!'

Both boys were waving their arms and doing funky moves.

'You fancy Jez!' Holly declared.

Rosanna denied it. 'You're dead!' she warned.

'Can we play musical cushions again?' Deanne asked when the Aaron Brown track had finished.

'No way! Keep dancing! This is cool!' was the verdict from every single person on the floor.

Even Perry was grooving.

'Here's an oldie but goldie from way back in the 1990s,' Gran announced. 'It's early Merlin Jones with his rap hit, "Everything About You"!'

'Wanna dance?' Justin asked Kayleigh. They were sitting in a quiet corner. He had his arm around her shoulder, and she was snuggled up close.

Kayleigh shook her head.

'You OK?' he asked.

She nodded.

'Sure you don't wanna dance?'

'Sure,' she murmured.

They sat and watched the kids instead.

'Not like that – like this!' Krystal was showing Carmel how to do her new dance sequence. 'Left foot forward, swing your right knee, bend your left leg and twist your shoulders. It's easy-peasy.'

Carmel tried to copy, but ended up in a heap.

'Dummy!' Krystal giggled.

'Everything-about-you-drives-me-wild, you're-a-hip-and-happening-crazy-child. I'm-your-man-and-that's-for-sure, for-what-I-feel-there-ain't-no-cure ...'

'Don't call me dummy!' Carmel grumbled.

'Well, you are,' Krystal retorted.

'Just because I don't spend hours in

front of a mirror practising.' Carmel sneered.

'I don't!'

'You do!'

'Don't!'

'Do!'

'And that was the fabulous Aaron Brown!'

As Gran switched tracks, Dad edged into the telly room. 'Everything OK in here?'

Gran nodded. 'We're rocking!'

Dad's eyes widened at the sight of Gran behind the CD player. 'Er – right!' he mumbled. Was this his own mother dee-jaying for a bunch of pre-teens? But then, nothing she ever did really surprised him. 'Maria and I thought we'd just take Kyle out in his pushchair for a breath of fresh air,' he told her.

'... Don't!' Krystal snapped for the fifth time.

'Do!' Carmel tried to outstare her, but failed. 'Anyway, who wants to do

your stupid dance!' she snorted,
stamping to the other side of the room.

'You go ahead!' Gran told David.

'You're sure we're not dropping you
in it?' he said nervously. Things were
pretty wild in here – bodies were
writhing, voices raised, faces red and
excited. In fact, he noticed that the
window was beginning to steam up a bit.

'Go!' Gran insisted. 'And don't hurry
back. Take it easy – we're having a
groovy time!'

So she was left in charge, playing
more tracks, bopping and grooving in
her silver-trimmed top and sparkling
earrings.

Carmel was still mad with Krystal.
From a safe distance she watched her
perfect her new routine, twizzling and
twirling in perfect time to the music.
'Mizz Disco-Diva!' she muttered under
her breath, wondering how she could
quickly even up the score. Then, when
her gaze fell on Perry, she saw how.

She zoomed across to Krystal and pulled her out of the dance. 'Perry Wade fancies you!' she hissed.

A look of horror swept over Krystal's face. 'He doesn't!'

'Does!'

'Doesn't! – How do you know?'

Carmel raised her eyebrows in a know-all way. 'He just told me.'

'Uh, that's gross!' Krystal groaned, backing off behind Carmel.

'He says he's gonna ask you to dance.'

Krystal stared at poor Perry, whose dancing style made him look like a chicken going round in
circles,
flapping its wings.

'Really gross!' Krystal said faintly.

Carmel hid a smirk. 'He really, really fancies you,' she insisted.

So Krystal took evasive action. She simply grabbed the nearest boy, who happened to be Danny, and started dancing with him before Perry had chance to make his move.

'I didn't know Krystal fancied Danny,' Jo-jo grumbled as she sidled up to Carmel. She was looking well miffed.

Carmel laughed. 'She doesn't. But I made her think Perry fancies her, and she *so* does not fancy Perry that she danced with Danny instead. But don't worry, Danny doesn't fancy Krystal, he fancies you!'

Jo-jo looked confused. Then she froze as Perry did his chicken-walk through the crowd towards her and Carmel. 'I'm outta here!' she gasped.

But Carmel wasn't quick enough.

'Er – Carmel – you wanna dance?' Perry mumbled.

She looked over her shoulder in

panic. 'Who, me?' she stammered.

Perry flapped his elbows. 'Yeah, you.'

'Go on, Carmel, dance!' Gran yelled above the music.

Everyone turned to stare at Carmel and Perry.

Carmel gulped. How had she got herself into this? Perry Wade, public enemy number one, who danced like a geek and only ever talked about megabytes and hard discs, was actually asking her, Carmel Wilde, to dance in front of everybody!

'Yeah, go on, Carmel, dance with Perry!' Krystal called as she grooved with cool Danny.

Carmel gulped once more then gritted her teeth. OK, she would show Krystal that she wasn't chicken – chicken, like Perry, ha ha! 'Yeah, all right,' she told him.

And Perry chicken-walked ahead of her into the middle of the floor.

*

'And we're winding down here at Hartland with one last track from Boyz R Us!' At five o'clock, Gran rounded off her groovy DJ stint.

Deanne went round with party poppers. *Pop-pop-pop!* Tiny coloured streamers exploded into the air and showered down. Some landed in Kayleigh's hair, and Justin carefully picked them out.

Tired dancers swayed and dragged their feet.

'I'm starving!' Bo cried as the last strains of Boyz R Us died away.

The boys scrummaged through the door into the kitchen to feast on leftovers. The girls followed to drink Pepsi.

As the others ate and drank, Carmel managed to corner Krystal by the sink. 'That was all your fault,' she began, her eyes screwed tight. 'You made me dance with Perry!'

'Not guilty!' Krystal shrugged. 'The

way I remember it, *you* were the one who tried to trick me into dancing with him.'

Since plucking up the courage to ask Carmel to dance, Perry had chicken-walked his way through every girl there, except Krystal. 'You're so jammy!' Carmel complained. 'He was jabbing me in the ribs with his elbows!'

Krystal sniffed. 'Yeah, I feel sorry for you – *not*!' Grazing among the leftover sandwiches and sausage rolls, she spied one lonely piece of birthday cake left on the plate and made a beeline for it.

But Carmel beat her to it, snatched the cake and held it out of reach.

'Hey, I saw that first!' Krystal cried.

'Didn't!'

'Did!'

Carmel held the plate high above her head, then

brought it sweeping down under Krystal's nose and out of reach again before Krystal could snatch it. 'Da-dah!'

'Act your age, you two,' Kayleigh said as she and Justin came into the kitchen hand in hand.

'It's mine!' Krystal claimed. 'I only had one piece earlier, and you had two!'

'Aah, diddums!' Carmel crowed.

Krystal lunged for the plate, but staggered into Deanne instead. Deanne toppled sideways into Justin, who over-balanced and stepped on Kayleigh's foot.

'Ouch!' Kayleigh hopped backwards with a high squeal.

'Give it to me!' Krystal demanded, charging Carmel and grabbing her around the waist.

Still Carmel kept the piece of cake out of reach. She opened her mouth and took a big bite. 'Tough!' she mumbled through the crumbs.

'For heaven's sake, it's only cake!' Kayleigh cried. Forgetting Justin, forgetting the fact that it was the twins' birthday, she snapped and launched into one of her famous wobblers. 'You two should be locked up and someone should throw away the key. You don't even *deserve* a party, the way you behave!'

Krystal let go of Carmel, who stopped mid-munch. 'Cool it,' they said.

It was like telling an avalanche to stop falling.

'You don't even deserve to breathe, you're both so horrible!' Kayleigh screeched. Events of the day had suddenly become too much – all the cake-making and icing, the demolition of the cake by Kyle, the rush to bring a stand-in one from Tesco's. 'You're always borrowing my stuff without asking. You fight all the time over nothing! And you've never ever, not once in your lives said thank you for anything!'

Carmel and Krystal stared at her in silence. OK, so Kayleigh could be bossy

and stop you going into her room
sometimes, but she hardly ever lost it
like this in public, and especially not
when Justin was around.

'Don't look at me like that!' she
stormed. Her neck was mottled red with
fury, her eyes flashed. 'I hate living
here with you two messing around and
scrapping over nothing. It drives me
crazy, I can't stand it!'

Carmel frowned and muttered under
her breath, something that sounded like,
'Same here.'

With a look that could kill, Kayleigh
snatched away the cake, flinging it
in the bin and turning back on the
attack. 'Finish! The end! Now no one
gets it.'

Krystal spread her hands, palms
upwards. 'Hold it. What did we do?'

'It's your birthday!' Kayleigh cried.
'Mum and Dad give you a cool party, and
what happens? You scrap over a stupid
piece of cake!'

'Oh, I get it – *you* wanted the cake,' Carmel said.

'Aaagh!' Kayleigh covered her face with her hands then looked up again. She drew herself up to her full height, turning to Justin and making an announcement with sudden icy calm. 'That's it, I'm out of here.'

'What d'you mean?' he asked.

Kayleigh took a deep breath and gave a tragic toss of her ponytail. 'I'm leaving this madhouse,' she declared. 'And I'm never, ever coming back!'

Six

'She'll get over it,' Carmel told Justin with a shrug.

The boyfriend stood and watched Kayleigh flounce off down the garden path.

'Yeah, she's always like this,' Krystal agreed. 'Give her half an hour and she'll be back.'

Kayleigh paused at the gate, glanced back then stormed on.

'That's Kayleigh for you,' Carmel tutted. 'Total drama queen.'

'W-w-where's she gone?' Justin stammered. One moment he'd been gently picking party poppers out of Kayleigh's hair, the next she'd been shrieking like the wicked witch of the north.

'Dunno. Don't care.' Krystal glowered into the bin at the last scraps of birthday cake. 'What a waste!'

Meanwhile, Carmel did a head count of who was left at the party. 'Where's Jade?' she asked, noticing for the first time that the skunk who'd invited Perry was nowhere to be seen. That left just Deanne, picking up party-popper streamers and draping them over her head.

'Jade's dead!' Krystal remembered.

'Everything-about-you-drives-me-wild, You're-a-hip-and-happening-crazy-child!' Deanne rapped, in a world of her own.

Amanda, Jo-jo, Holly and Rosanna were back in the telly room, hanging out with the boys and laughing at their jokes.

'I'd better go after her,' Justin
decided, plucking up the courage to
follow Kayleigh.

'Best not,' Carmel advised. 'I'd wait
for her to calm down if I were you.'

'Yeah, when she's like this, she's
mad, bad and dangerous to know,'
Krystal agreed darkly.

The garden gate swung on its hinges.
A number 62 bus trundled by.

Justin took a deep breath. He closed
his eyes and psyched himself up. 'I'm
gonna find her!' he muttered.

Carmel and Krystal watched him jog
down the path, pick up his bike and
pedal off.

'That's true *lurve*!' Krystal shrugged.

'Madness,' Carmel agreed with a
bewildered sigh.

'Did you see that?' Jade asked Hamlet,
holding him up to the shed window
to give him a back view of Kayleigh
storming up the path.

The hamster's cheeks were stuffed with bird food, he was feeling sleepy and content.

'That's my big sis. She looks like she's in one of her strops – you can tell by the way she just slammed the gate. Y'see that crop-top she's wearing? She got it at Top Shop in the sale. It's cool.'

Chobble-chobble-chomp. Hamlet concentrated on chewing and swallowing.

'Your feet tickle my hand, did you know that?' Jade told him. 'Perry's dead lucky to have a pet, and dead mean not to let me borrow you.'

Jade glanced round the Wades' shed at the neat stacks of empty plant pots and rows of garden tools. Hamlet's cage stood on a shelf above the lawn mower, next to an old, upturned washing-up bowl. 'We've got a shed like this in our garden,' she muttered to herself. 'You could easily come and stay with us for a bit.'

Chobble-scratch-chobble. Hamlet was

waking up a bit, stretching and
scratching, ready for action.

'Don't – that tickles!'
Scratch-wriggle-wiggle.
'No, that really does
tickle!' Jade gasped,
feeling Hamlet squirm.
Out of the corner of her
eye she saw Justin run
out of her house, grab
his bike and cycle after
Kayleigh. Wow, perhaps
he and Kayleigh had just had a mega
row! What had she missed? 'Gotta go,'
she told Hamlet, making a move to
plonk him back in his cage.

Wriggle-twist! No way was the
hamster ready to go back behind bars.
He turned a somersault then back-
flipped out of Jade's hands.

'Eek!' Jade felt him slip through
her fingers and saw him land on the
washing-up bowl. She made a grab for
him, missed and panicked as the bowl

fell on to the lawn mower and Perry's pet disappeared behind the plant pots. 'Oh, no!'

What now? Jade's mind went into overdrive. *What if the hamster hurt himself on one of the sharp garden tools? What if he fell from the shelf and broke a leg?*

'Hamlet, here boy!' she hissed, picking up plastic pots and knocking packets of seeds to the floor.

What if he fell and skewered himself on the spikes of the rake? Or chomped the slug-pellets in the container standing in a dark corner? He could die of poison, and it would be all her fault. She, wicked Jade Wilde, would be to blame for the death of a poor, innocent hamster!

Mega-big panic! Starting to sweat, Jade searched the shelves, knocking off a ball of garden string, which unravelled and got caught up around her feet. *Rats!*

Hamlet sat quietly behind a watering can. His little black eyes glittered.

Jade looked under a pair of thick

gloves, then inside an empty wooden box. Nothing! Hamlet had vanished.

Of course, he could move pretty darn quick – Jade didn't know a lot about hamsters, but she knew this much. And now she realized with a start that the shed door was hanging open – like, *wide* open! And out there was blue sky, green trees, grass – in a word, freedom!

What had there been to stop Hamlet somersaulting out of her hands, on to the floor and straight out of the door? Gone, just like that!

A cold shiver ran down Jade's spine. Her legs went weak at the knees. With one last look at the chaos around her, and with fear in her heart, she legged it from Perry Wade's shed.

'No, no, don't you hurry back!' Gran was saying to David and Maria as the twins' party wound down with one last game of musical cushions. She spoke into the phone above the sound of Merlin Jones's rap hit. 'Everything's fine here,' she trilled. 'You stay where you are and have a nice chat with your friend. How's Kyley? Still asleep, bless! Well, make the most of it while I hold the fort back here.'

'I'm-your-man-and-that's-for-sure. For-what-I-feel-there-ain't-no-cure ...' Deanne rapped out of the telly room into the hall. 'Krystal and Carmel are having a cushion fight,' she whispered.

Gran put down the phone and waded in.

Whack! Krystal landed a cushion blow on Carmel's shoulder. 'You were out!' she yelled. 'I won the prize 'cos I was the last one left!'

Smack! Carmel returned the blow. 'Cheat!'

'Not!'

'Are!'

'Girls!' Gran said, cutting in between them and yanking the cushions from their grasp. 'I'm the referee, and I say no one gets a prize!'

'B-but!'

''S not fair!'

'That's my final answer,' Gran insisted, looking around for help. 'Who was in charge while I was on the phone? Where's Kayleigh?'

'Gone,' Carmel said shortly. She noticed that while she and Krystal had been fighting over cushions, Jo-jo and Danny had holed up in a corner with Jez and Amanda, and that Holly and Rosanna were getting on well with Mark and Bo. *Hmmm.*

'Where's that nice, fair-haired boy?' Gran asked.

'Justin left too,' Krystal told her. She ducked behind Deanne when she saw Perry heading her way.

Perry swerved and pounced on Carmel instead. 'You wanna come next door and see my hamster, Carmel?'

'Whoo-oooh!' Krystal sniggered.

'I'm not Carmel, I'm Krystal,' Carmel lied. She enjoyed the look of confusion on Perry's face.

'OK, er – Krystal then. D'you wanna see Hamlet?'

'No way!'

'Aaaah!' Jo-jo led the loud chorus. 'Go and see Perry's hamster, don't be mean!'

At that moment Jade burst in through the back door. Her hair was a mess, her face was hot and sweaty, and there was a trail of green string around her ankle.

'Where have you been?' Carmel demanded, breaking away from Perry.

Jade caught her breath. 'Nowhere.'

'Where's nowhere? You missed our party.' Krystal joined in. People were drifting off in pairs, saying thanks to Gran and bye to the twins.

'Great party,' Jo-jo said, hand in hand with cool Danny.

'Yeah, thanks for inviting us,' Bo grinned.

'We didn't!' Krystal sniffed and tossed her head.

By now only Perry was hanging on, looking sad and left out, until Deanne stepped in. 'Can I come and see your hamster?' she asked him.

The word *hamster* sent a shock wave through Jade. As Deanne went off with Perry, she dived into the kitchen and sat down on a stool, her hands shaking, her throat dry.

'Bye, dear! Bye-bye!' Gran was busy waving people off at the front door. Soon only Krystal, Carmel and Jade were left.

'OK, so where were you?' Krystal insisted, pinning Jade back against a cupboard.

'In – in the park!' Jade gasped lamely. Suddenly her talent for fibbing

seemed to have
fled.

'Yeah, right!'
Stooping to
unravel the
string from
around Jade's
ankle, Carmel
held it up.
'Where were you
really?'

Jade squinted
at the string. 'What's it to you?' she
grunted.

Krystal and Carmel eyed her fiercely.
'Look, you're already dead for inviting
Perry to the party,' Carmel reminded
Jade. 'I had to dance with him!

'Yeah, you're dead. So where've you
been?' Krystal demanded.

'Nowhere. Where's Mum and Dad?
Where's Kyle? Where's Kayleigh?' Jade
fired questions back at the twins. She
stared round at the wreckage – dirty

cups and plates, half-eaten sandwiches, empty party-poppers.

'Oh yeah, Kayleigh.' Suddenly Carmel backed off and sat down. 'I'd forgotten about that.'

'She threw a wobbler,' Krystal told Jade.

'So?' To Jade this was nothing new. Anyway, she'd seen her older sister storming off with her own eyes.

'We mean a major one,' Carmel insisted. Now that she thought about it, this left them with a bit of a problem. 'What are we gonna tell Mum and Dad when they get back?' she asked Krystal. 'Like, "Mum, we're sorry but we upset Kayleigh and she left in a major bad mood. Now we don't know where she is."'

'We don't have to say we upset her,' Krystal pointed out.

'But people heard. Justin saw it all,' Carmel reminded her. 'He's bound to dob us in.'

'Sounds like you're the ones who are in deep doo-doo,' Jade pointed out, glad to shift the attention away from Perry Wade's shed and the Houdini hamster. 'What happened exactly?'

'Nothing!' Krystal and Carmel clammed up.

'Come on. Kayleigh had a major strop. What else?'

Action replay: the twins remembered Kayleigh grabbing the last bit of cake and chucking it in the bin. 'She said we were horrible,' Carmel muttered.

'Right.' *No argument there,* Jade thought. 'Then what?'

'She said she hated living here,' Krystal admitted.

This was starting to sound serious. Jade snuck over to close the door so Gran couldn't hear. 'Cool!' she whispered, forgetting Hamlet for the moment. This Kayleigh thing sounded much more exciting. 'Then what?'

Carmel frowned uncomfortably at

Krystal. 'Then she said she was leaving this madhouse.'

'Leaving?' Jade squeaked. She cleared her throat. 'Leaving? How? What? When? Why?'

'For ever,' Krystal said in a hollow voice. She remembered the angry flick of Kayleigh's ponytail and Justin's horrified expression. 'And she said she's never, ever – that means *never* – coming back!'

Seven

Wow! Major drama. Kayleigh had left
home! Jade's eyes almost popped out
of her head. 'Exciting, or what!' she
gasped.

'Yeah, and it was down to us,' Carmel
agreed, not sure now whether to feel
guilty or proud.

'Five Wilde sisters hanging on a wall ...!'
Jade sang, to the tune of 'Ten Green
Bottles'. 'Five Wilde sisters hanging on
a wall. And if one Wilde sister should
accidentally fall ...'

'There'd be *four* Wilde sisters da-di-da-
di-dah!' Krystal chimed in.

'Sssh! Gran doesn't know,' Carmel reminded them.

And in any case, they were forced to change the subject when Deanne came running back from Perry's house.

'Eek!' she said, waving her arms like a windmill. 'Eek! Help! Oh no!'

At first Krystal thought Deanne was doing one of her famous animal impressions. After all, Deanne had been known to spend a whole week perfecting the art of being Skippy the kangaroo. 'Are you a mouse?' she guessed. 'Or a rat? No, don't tell me – you're a hamster!'

'Hamsters don't make noises,' Carmel frowned.

Deanne had begun to jump up and down and nod her head at the word 'hamster'. 'Help!' she squeaked, arms waving madly. 'Help! Perry! Eek!'

Carmel and Krystal pounced and pinned her down. 'What about Perry?'

'Come quick,' Deanne gasped, dragging them out and down the lawn.

Bummer! Jade swallowed hard. This party was so not what a party should be. Sisters were leaving home. Boys were showing up who hadn't been invited. Hamsters were escaping!

'Jade, come with us!' Carmel yelled over her shoulder.

I so do not want to do that! she thought. But then how bad would that look? 'Yeah, coming!' she sighed, slamming the kitchen door behind her.

'Perry?' Carmel approached with caution.

She and Krystal had found him sitting on his shed floor surrounded by plant-pots, packets of seed, plastic bags and unravelled string. He was covered in dust, there were streaks of half-dried tears on his cheeks.

'Eek!' Deanne cried. 'Help him!'

'We will once we find out what happened,' Krystal told her with a frown. Those tears were a deeply worrying sign that their geeky neighbour

was human after all. 'Stand up, Perry,'
she said sharply. 'Tell us what's wrong.'

'H-h-hamster,' he stammered,
pointing to the empty cage on the shelf.

'Yeah, Jade said you had a hamster,'
encouraged Carmel.

'*Had*,' he said in a hollow voice.

Then the twins spotted the cage door
hanging open. 'The hamster legged it?'
Krystal gasped.

Perry got unsteadily to his feet. 'I
came to show Deanne. But when we got
here, the whole place was wrecked. The
cage door was open, and ...'

Oh, no, he was going to blub again!
Not that! Anything but that! Quickly
Carmel took charge. 'Listen, Perry – er,
Pez – we wanna help, but we need to
know more. Like, what colour is it? Is it
a he or a she? When did you last see it?
That kind of detective type stuff.'

Meanwhile, Krystal spotted Jade
hanging about by the hedge. 'He's got a
hamster, but it's legged it!' she reported.

Jade coloured up. 'So?'

'We're gonna help him find it.'
Krystal tilted her head to one side.
Tick-tick-tick – her brain began to click
into action. *Hamster – garden shed –
plant pots – green string ...*

Jade could see that Krystal was
thinking hard, putting two and two
together and quickly making four. 'I'm
off to look for Kayleigh!' she gabbled,
making a beeline for the
gap in the hedge.

But Krystal blocked
her way with a
slick karate move.
'Hah!' she cried.
'Green string! You
came back just
now with green
string round your ankle!'

'So?'

'So!' With more Kung-Fu moves,
slicing her hands through the air and
kicking out with her right foot, Krystal

advanced. 'You, Jade, know about ham-stair!' she said in a heavy foreign accent. 'You come, see ham-stair in shed. You let him es-cape. Hah-so!'

'You're mad,' Jade growled. Wow, this party was so not working out!

'... Chocolate brown.' Inside Perry's shed, Carmel was memorizing details about Hamlet. 'How big?'

'This big.' Perry trod on empty pots and crunched them underfoot. He searched behind the lawn mower for at least the tenth time.

'Listen!' Krystal cornered Jade. 'This is the deal. Carmel and I will keep quiet about you and the hamster ...'

'There's nothing to keep quiet about!' Jade argued furiously. But it was no good, the green string could be used in evidence against her!

'We won't dob you in about the hamster if you don't dob Carmel and me in about Kayleigh! And you help us look for them both!'

'Hmm,' Jade grimaced.

'C'mon, let's get to work,' Carmel was telling Perry, dragging him into the garden, ready for action. 'The longer we wait, the more chance Hamlet has of being chewed by a cat or squished by a bus. We've got to get a move on here!'

Perry cringed and almost cried again, then pulled himself together.

'Deal?' Krystal hissed at Jade.

I so wish I was ... somewhere else! Jade thought. 'Deal!' she muttered.

Swish! went the dishwasher. *Swish-slurp-gurgle-hisssss!*

'You lived your life like a candle in the wind!' Gran sang. 'Never knowing who to turn to when the wind came in ... !'

'Rain!' Carmel told her. 'When the *rain* came in!'

Gran was clearing the party wreck-age, stacking plates, wiping surfaces, filling bin-bags with wrapping-paper, envelopes, streamers and burst balloons.

'I would've liked to know you ... !' Gran trilled. 'But I was just a kid ...'

Carmel was quietly collecting the items a good detective needed on the trail of a missing hamster – paper, pen, blu-tak, muesli ...

'I'd like to have the house spick and span for when your mum and dad get back,' Gran told her cheerily. 'They bumped into their friend Mick while they were out, so they're having a nice chat at his house.'

'When will they come home?' Carmel asked casually, ferreting to find out how long they had before people started to worry about where Kayleigh was.

Gran glanced at her watch. 'In a couple of hours, maybe. Why?'

'Nothing. It doesn't matter. Bye!' *Whoosh!* Carmel was out of the door.

Carmel, Krystal and Deanne wrote the notices in bright felt tip. Sad Perry blu-tacked them to the trees and lampposts.

'Did you tell your mum yet?' Jade asked anxiously, knowing that Perry's mother could be dead scary. OK, so she wore high heels and tight tops, but when she came at you with an egg whisk, you ran!

Perry shook his head sadly. 'She's gone shopping. Dad's upstairs watching tennis on the telly.' He went on and posted more notices about his beloved missing pet.

'Perry, will you stop being so ... !' Jade begged.

'... Pathetic,' Krystal suggested, putting the top on her felt tip.

'... Tragic,' Carmel sniffed. After all, they had enough problems of their own to worry about.

'... SAD!' Jade cried.

'Lost'
one Hamster
NAME: HAMLET
Colour: DARKISH
Telephone
67512

But he couldn't help it. His face was
pale, his eyes bleary when he thought of
Hamlet's empty cage.

'I'll look in the
shed again!' Deanne
offered, seizing the
bag of muesli and
scurrying off.

Meanwhile,
Krystal, Jade and
Carmel tried to
persuade Perry
that their notices
would do the trick.

'You have to wait
by your phone,' Krystal told him. 'Don't
move, OK? If someone rings to say
they've found Hamlet, you have to be
there to take the call.'

'What are you going to do?' he asked
miserably.

'We're gonna look for Kay— erm,
Hamlet, of course!' Carmel said. They
were down to about an hour and a half

before Mum and Dad got back
and kicked up a fuss about Kayleigh.
And they could hardly blu-tak notices
to the bus-stop saying, 'LOST – ONE
SISTER!'

Getting rid of Perry at last, Krystal
and Carmel turned on Jade. They were
on the pavement, dragging out of her
the facts about what had actually
happened inside Perry's shed when
Justin reappeared at the top of the
street.

Jade dodged around the bus shelter
and ran to meet Justin. 'Give me some
good news. Did you find Kayleigh?'

But Justin shook his head. 'I've
looked everywhere – the park, town –
everywhere.'

'Bummer!'

'I'm really worried about her.'

'Don't be,' Jade told him. 'Kayleigh's
tough. She can look after herself.'

'But she'd totally lost it. I don't
think she knew what she was doing.'

Justin spoke quietly, as if re-running
the whole ugly scene.

'Yeah, she often flips. One time
Krystal borrowed her *Teen Dream* without
asking. Krystal only wanted to read her
horo— horror— horri— her stars, but
Kayleigh went nuts. She didn't speak to
any of us for a whole week.' Which had
been a relief, if Jade was to admit
the truth. Which she didn't often, and
wasn't about to now.

Anyway, Justin wasn't listening.
'Where could she have gone?' he
wondered. His legs were tired from
pedalling, his brain tied up in knots
of worry.

So Jade thought back to the moment
when Kayleigh had stomped out of the
house, up the garden path.

Wham! The gate had slammed shut.
Kayleigh's fair ponytail had swished, her
head had vanished behind the hedge.
That would be right about here, where
Jade was standing now. Kayleigh Wilde,

thirteen years old, dressed in a green crop-top and navy blue cut-offs, last seen here by the number 62 bus stop.

'Hey!' Jade gasped.

It was a cry that brought Krystal and Carmel running.

Slam! Swish! Vanish! Justin had raced after his girlfriend on his bike. He should easily have overtaken her if she was on foot. But what if she wasn't? What if she'd chosen some other form of transport?

'That's it!' Jade cried.

Justin and the twins stared at her in silence.

'There was one going by just as Kayleigh stormed off. I've just remembered, it was stopping at the stop! That's totally, definitely it!'

Justin gawped. Carmel frowned. Krystal threatened Jade with a karate chop. 'One what? Spit it out!' she demanded.

So Jade explained. 'Think about it.

Kayleigh leaves home. She's never
coming back. But you know her –
when did you ever see her walk
anywhere if she can get a lift?'

'True,' Krystal agreed. Kayleigh
definitely won the world record for *not*
walking.

'So?' Carmel asked.

'So, she gets to the gate and thinks,
gosh, what am I doing? This leaving
home stuff is too much like hard work!'
Jade paused to tap the side of the see-
through bus shelter. 'Then she sees one
of these coming, and that's the answer.
No need to walk after all!'

'You mean?' Carmel's frown slowly
disappeared.

'She ... ?' Krystal hesitated.

Jade nodded. 'Kayleigh left home on
a number 62 bus!'

Eight

'Think about it!' Jade urged. 'Kayleigh's on the bus. She doesn't have to walk anywhere, so she's happy.'

Justin nodded. 'Yeah, I did see a bus driving off up the street. I rode the opposite way, so I didn't notice who was on it.'

Slowly the twins agreed that Jade might be right. 'Why didn't you mention this before?' Carmel wanted to know, as if everything was her fault, as usual.

Jade glowered back. '"Thanks, Jade, for being so brainy and working it all out!"' she quipped.

'Whoa-whoa-whoa!' Justin didn't want any more Wilde arguments. Instead, he got down to business. 'Where does the number 62 go to from here?

'Into town, and then out to High Hartsbridge,' Krystal said.

Justin tried to picture what Kayleigh would have done once the bus had reached the end of its journey. 'What's out there?'

Krystal shrugged. 'Nothing. High Hartsbridge is an itty-bitty village in the middle of nowhere.' No discos, no clothes shops. Kayleigh would soon be bored out of her tiny mind.

Yet again, it was Jade who thought things through. 'Hang on, there's a place where people take donkeys that no one wants – donkey santinary.'

'Sanctuary,' Carmel interrupted.

Jade ignored her. 'We've been there with Gran, when she goes to help. It's cool.'

'Yeah, but Kayleigh wouldn't go

there,' Krystal pointed out. 'Too smelly and dirty.'

Jade sighed impatiently. 'I know that, dummy! But what I'm saying to Justin is, we know the village 'cos that's where Gran lives.'

Justin nodded and listened.

Jade spelt things out. 'Gran lives at number 6 Old Bridge Lane. So, Kayleigh jumps on the number 62 and rides until she gets to the stop right outside Gran's house. Then she hops off. She only has to walk a few metres up the path, then use Gran's spare key which is hidden under a stone by the water barrel in the back garden. There's nobody home 'cos Gran's busy here. Kayleigh lets herself in and turns on the telly.'

'Then what?' Justin asked.

'Then nothing.' Jade tried to explain that catching a bus was more than enough effort for Kayleigh in one day. 'She knows we're panicking while she's sitting with her feet up. That's good

enough for her. Eventually Gran will
arrive home and Kayleigh will give her
this big sob story about Krystal and
Carmel being ungrateful little pigs—'

'Hey, who are you calling a pig?'
Carmel and Krystal challenged.

'... Gran will cheer her up then call
Mum. Mum will persuade Kayleigh to
come back home and then she'll ground
these two for ever.'

'End of story?' Justin checked.

Krystal nodded. 'It's our birthday and
we're gonna get grounded!'

'Unless ...' Carmel cut in, suddenly
alert. She'd spied a bus at the bottom
of the street. It lurched towards them,
signalling to pull in at the stop.

Krystal tuned in to what she was
thinking. '... Unless we get to her first!'

The bus driver drew to a halt as
Krystal finished her sentence.

'Right!' Jade agreed. 'Let's do it!'

And without another word, Jade,
Carmel and Krystal hopped on the bus.

*

'Here, Hamlet! Here, Hammy-Hammy!'
Deanne rootled around in Perry's shed
amongst the big wellies and coils of
plastic hose. She went down on to her
hands and knees, poking in dark corners.

Inside the house, Perry sat forlornly
by the silent telephone.

'No, not you, Mr Spider!' Deanne
tutted, when a big one with brown blobs
on his pale, fat body crept out from
behind the lawn mower to investigate.
So far she'd found five live spiders and
two dead bluebottles, but no hamster.
However, she had seen small scuff marks
on the dusty floorboards, and even a
hole chewed in the corner of one of
the packets of seeds – recent signs of
hamster for sure!

'And not you either, Mrs Bee!' Deanne
ducked to avoid a low-flying bumblebee
which had lost its way and flown into
the shed. Now it buzzed at the closed
window in angry spurts. 'That way!'

Deanne ordered, wafting it back out through the open door.

It was then that she saw Mrs Wade coming home from her shopping trip. Their neighbour was loaded down with half a dozen shiny carrier bags, calling at Perry through the window to open the door for her.

After a while Perry did as he was told, glancing out past his mum at Deanne. 'Did you find him yet?' he mouthed silently.

Deanne shook her head.

Perry's shoulders sagged as his mum battled her way through the door with her bags.

'Here, Hammy!' Deanne said again, her fist full of muesli. 'Nice, yummy food! Here, boy!'

OK, did I blow it with Justin? Kayleigh asked herself. She was staring at the telly in Gran's lounge, not taking in any of the ancient movie she was watching.

Let's run through this one more time.

I lose it big-time with the twins while Justin is standing there. Krystal and Carmel are well out of order, but me losing it is not a pretty sight. And he was staring at me like I was a loonie, I remember that.

Pursing her lips and fiddling nervously with her fingernails, Kayleigh felt sure that the romance with her gorgeous Tesco's fitster was history.

I can't blame him really, she admitted to herself. *I was a bit – well, loud. And boys scare easily. Yeah, there was that haunted look in his eyes, and he didn't say a word or try to stop me. He just let me storm off. Yeah, we're history,* she decided, turning up the volume to drown out her sorrows.

Justin set off on his bike from the Wilde house. He didn't follow the bus that Jade, Krystal and Carmel had got on. Instead, he took short cuts through the town and out the other side. Soon he was on a country road, pedalling like crazy.

OK, so it had been a bit of a surprise when Kayleigh had lost her cool. In fact, it was a total shock – that gobsmacking, mind-blowing transformation. And yeah, it was scary – the very fact that she could yell and scream like that, for a start, never mind the vicious things she said. But hey, he did have a thirteen-year-old girl cousin of his own, and so he knew a bit about them and their moods. Also, Kayleigh was really pretty.

Reaching the top of a hill, Justin looked down on a village in the valley below. There was a river running through it, and just a small row of houses and a pub next to an old stone bridge. Plucking up courage, he swooped down the hill.

'The wheels on the bus go round and round!' Jade hummed.

'Shut up, Jade!' Krystal and Carmel snapped. Time was running out. If they didn't get to Kayleigh soon and persuade her to come back before Mum and Dad got home, the birthday girls were in big trouble.

The bus rattled along past Tesco's on the outskirts of town, along the main road, then left up a steep hill. The road grew narrower and the lane rougher.

'All day long!' Jade chirruped. 'Look, there's the sancti-thingy!' She pointed into the valley at donkeys grazing happily in big green fields.

Krystal clenched her fists and spoke

in a mumble. 'What if Kayleigh refuses
to listen?'

Rattle-sway-bump! The bus lurched on.

'You know what she's like!' Krystal
insisted. 'She could still be in a massive
mood.'

'*If* she's even here!' Carmel warned.
She too was feeling jittery. 'Some
birthday party this turned out to be!'
she groaned.

But Jade sat at the front and hummed
her way through the rhyme, with
matching actions. 'The horn on the bus
goes honk-honk-honk! ... All day long!'

The knock on Gran's door nearly made
Kayleigh jump out of her skin.

'Climb every mountain!' a nun sang
on the telly. 'Ford every stream!'

'Who's there?' Kayleigh asked,
trotting up to the door and trying to
peer out of the letterbox.

'Follow every by-way ...' the nun
warbled.

'It's me!' Justin whispered. He could just see Kayleigh's nose and one eye through the slit.

Kayleigh gasped and sat down on the floor.

'... Till you find your dream!'

'Kayleigh?' Justin inquired. What happened? Had she fainted, or scarpered, or what?

'Yeah, hang on!' Staggering to her feet, Kayleigh searched frantically for the key then opened the door.

'You OK?' he asked. Her eyes were red, her face was blotchy.

He stood in the doorway, hair blown by the wind, slightly out of breath, his bike ditched at the front gate. 'I am now!' Kayleigh said, falling into his arms.

'Kayleigh, you gotta come home!' Krystal burst into Gran's house without knocking, with Carmel and Jade hard on her heels.

'I am sixteen, going on seventeen,' a

blonde girl sang on the telly.

'Kayleigh?' Carmel cannoned into the back of Krystal, then Jade bumped into the back of her.

Kayleigh and Justin were locked together on Gran's sofa.

'Innocent as a lamb ...' the actress sang, in the arms of her screen lover.

'Justin!' Krystal cried.

The real life romantics sprang to their feet. Justin cleared his throat, Kayleigh smoothed her hair.

'How did you get here so fast?'

'What's going on?'

'Is she still mad?'

Jade, Krystal and Carmel bombarded Justin with questions.

Kayleigh stepped forward. 'Yeah, "she" is still mad!' she insisted, looking ready for a fight.

The three girls gritted their teeth and waited for the next torrent of abuse.

But Justin grinned. 'She's not really,' he assured them. 'She's just glad you're here.'

Kayleigh hesitated and glanced at him. 'I am?' she queried.

'You are,' he said firmly, sliding his arm around her waist.

Kayleigh took a big breath. 'I am!' she agreed.

'You are?' Krystal and Carmel couldn't believe their ears.

It took Jade to get things clear. 'So you won't tell Mum about the twins having a mega fight? And you'll come home with us before Mum and Dad get back?'

'No, and yes,' Kayleigh said, sweet as pie. She gazed up into Justin's eyes.

'I am seventeen, going on eighteen,' the blond boy in uniform sang on the telly to his innocent-as-a-lamb girlfriend. 'I-I'll take ca-are of you!'

It was dusk. Birds were singing and swallows were soaring through a pinkish sky.

'You're amazing!' Maria Wilde told Gran. 'How did you manage to get the house so clean so quickly?'

Gran beamed and winked. 'Did you have a nice time with your friend?' she asked back.

Jade, Kayleigh, Carmel and Krystal watched Mum hand a sleeping Kyle over to Dad, who took him upstairs to bed. They were still breathless from their quick scoot back home.

'Don't push your luck!' Kayleigh had warned the others on the return bus journey. 'I'll keep quiet this time, because I promised Justin. But next time you act like hooligans, I'll get you grounded for a year!'

Carmel and Krystal grinned. 'Thank you, Justin!' they'd breathed.

And now here he was, riding up on his bike, to join them at home.

'What a lovely evening!' Gran smiled, looking out at the shepherd's delight sky. 'The perfect end to a perfect day!'

The twins' grins broadened. 'Yeah, thanks for a cool party!' they chimed.

'Thanks, Mum and Dad. Thanks, Gran!'

'And were the birthday girls good?' Dad asked.

There was a long pause. Kayleigh looked like she'd swallowed a whole lemon, but she didn't say a word.

'They were fine!' Gran said.

Phew! Krystal glanced sideways at Carmel.

'And what about you, Jade?' Mum turned to the figure hanging around in the background. 'Did you manage to stay out of trouble?'

Jade bit her bottom lip. Unluckily for her, she'd just seen Mrs Wade and Perry heading their way. This was a last-minute hitch she could have done without.

'Maria!' Maggie Wade minced up the path in her high heels, with Perry tagging behind.

'Uh-oh!' Krystal and Carmel cringed.

But Deanne appeared out of
nowhere, her hands closely cupped in
front of her. *Eek!*

'Oh Maria, your little Deanne is so
clever!' Maggie Wade began.

Jade saw that Perry was ... smiling.
Yeah, definitely grinning from ear to ear!

'Poor Perry lost his hamster.
Apparently he was cleaning Hamlet's cage
and the pesky little thing ran away!'

Woah, thanks, Perry! Jade breathed
again.

'Perry searched and searched. Your
girls broke off from their party and
helped him put notices on the trees,
which was very kind!' Just for a second,
Mrs Wade paused for breath.

'Eek!' Deanne squeaked, offering to
show Jade what she was carrying.

Jade peeked between Deanne's
fingers. She saw a pair of black, beady
eyes and two fat, furry cheeks.

'And then Deanne came and turned
our whole shed upside down. It was

her who found the little runaway!'

'Wicked!' Jade breathed.

Deanne beamed and squeaked.
'Hamlet likes muesli!' she announced.

Thank you, Deanne! Thank you, Perry!
For the first time in her life, Jade was
forced to feel grateful to their geeky
neighbour.

So it all turned out OK in the end.

Kayleigh and Justin had gone off all
lovey-dovey to his house. Gran had
caught the bus back home. Perry had
put Hamlet safely back in his cage, with
a promise that he wouldn't tell a soul
about what had really happened. Deanne
had gone to bed early with a book on
how to take care of hamsters.

'That was a mega day!' Krystal sighed
over the pile of presents up in her room.

'Cool!' Carmel agreed, reading
through her cards.

Jade overheard them talking and
popped her head around the door. 'You

know why Perry kept quiet?' she asked, with a twinkle in her eye.

'No, why?' Carmel and Krystal asked.

'He told me it's because he fancies you!' she crowed.

The twins looked shocked. 'Which one?' they cried.

'Both of you!' Jade laughed, dodging out of sight.

Carmel and Krystal shot after her. 'Jade Wilde, you're dead!' they yelled through her closed door.

'Waaaagh!' Kyle woke up with a start. 'Waaa-aaa-aaagh – *choke* – *splutter*!'

'You're definitely, one hundred per cent dead!' the twins swore.

Just the end of another ordinary day in the life of the Wilde family.